THE WA

 *Get set with a Read Alone!*

This entertaining series is designed for all new readers who want to start reading a whole book on their own.

Read Alones may be two or three short stories in one book, or one longer story with chapters, so they are ideal for building reading confidence.

The stories are lively and fun, with lots of illustrations and clear, large type, to make first solo reading a perfect pleasure!

Some other Read Alones for you to enjoy

CLASS 1 SPELLS TROUBLE Margaret Nash
DUSTBIN CHARLIE Ann Pilling
GERTIE'S GANG Margaret Joy
POOR LITTLE MARY Kathryn Cave
ROSA AND HER SINGING GRANDFATHER
　　Leon Rosselson
SIMON'S MAGIC BOBBLE HAT Bill Bevan
THERE'S A TROLL AT THE BOTTOM OF
　　MY GARDEN Ann Jungman
THREE LITTLE FUNNY ONES
　　Charlotte Hough
THE TWIG THING Jan Mark

Alexander McCall Smith

The Watermelon Boys

Illustrated by Lis Toft

VIKING

This book is for Charlotte Lynn

VIKING

Published by the Penguin Group
Penguin Books Ltd, 27 Wrights Lane, London W8 5TZ, England
Penguin Books USA Inc., 375 Hudson Street, New York, New York 10014, USA
Penguin Books Australia Ltd, Ringwood, Victoria, Australia
Penguin Books Canada Ltd, 10 Alcorn Avenue, Toronto, Ontario, Canada M4V 3B2
Penguin Books (NZ) Ltd, 182–190 Wairau Road, Auckland 10, New Zealand

Penguin Books Ltd, Registered Offices: Harmondsworth, Middlesex, England

First published 1996
10 9 8 7 6 5 4 3 2 1

First edition

Typeset in 18/24 Times New Roman Schoolbook

Made and printed in Great Britain by Butler & Tanner Ltd, Frome and London

A CIP catalogue record for this book is available from the British Library

ISBN 0-670-86407-2

0670 864 072 5307

Chapter One

Have you ever eaten a watermelon? If you have, you will know what they are like. They are large and round, green on the outside, but red and juicy inside. On a hot

day, when the sun is burning
high in the sky, a watermelon
is one of the best things to
cool you down.

Misipo and his friend Sepo
loved watermelons. Whenever
they were given a little bit of

money for some chore they
had done, they would buy a
watermelon with it. They
bought them from an old
woman they knew called Ma
Rosie. She had a field full of
fine watermelons a little way

out of town.

The old lady grew the watermelons by herself. This she did very well, even though she was bent with age and had to use a stick to help her walk.

One Saturday Misipo was given a few coins for cleaning his uncle's shoes especially well. It was a hot day, and of course he thought that a watermelon would be a good idea.

"May I go to Ma Rosie's?" Misipo asked his parents. "I should like to buy a watermelon."

Misipo's mother and father agreed. They knew Ma Rosie well, and they were always happy for him to visit her.

Misipo went off to fetch his best friend Sepo first. Sepo

couldn't wait to share a watermelon, and so off the two boys went to Ma Rosie's. It was quite a long walk, and by the time they reached her house they were both looking forward to a cool and juicy watermelon.

Ma Rosie was sitting in her doorway, her head sunk in her hands. This was very unusual for her. The boys sensed immediately that something was wrong.

"Has something happened?" asked Misipo as he went up to the door.

Ma Rosie looked up. She had been crying, and her cheeks were still wet with tears.

"The man who usually buys my watermelons came today," she said. "He told me that he

doesn't want to buy them any more. He says that he has found a place where he can get them much cheaper."

Misipo felt angry.

"But your watermelons are by far the best watermelons in town!" he protested. "Surely he knows that!"

Ma Rosie shook her head.

"I told him that," she said. "But he wouldn't listen. He said that his mind has been made up.

"Nobody wants to buy my watermelons now," she went on. "All the watermelon growers these days take their

own watermelons to market.
But I'm too weak to walk that
far. I can't do that."

Misipo and Sepo stayed
with Ma Rosie for a while

and tried to cheer her up. But
however hard they tried, Ma
Rosie still seemed sad.
Eventually they left her where
they had found her, alone on
her doorstep.

"We must think of some

way to help," said Misipo.
"We can't let this happen to
Ma Rosie."

Sepo agreed. But what
could they do? They could not
buy all her watermelons
themselves. And it would be

impossible to take them all to market for her. If she could not sell them, then she would have to give up her field.

They walked home in silence, each racking his brains for an idea. Then, just as they were

almost home, Misipo stopped
and turned to Sepo.

"I know what we can do,"
he said. "My uncle used to sell
ice-creams at the hotel. We

could try to sell Aunt Rosie's watermelons there. We could cut them into slices and sell them to the guests!"

"What a wonderful idea!" said Sepo. "Let's go and talk

to Ma Rosie about it
tomorrow."

"I'm sure it'll work," said
Misipo. "I wonder why
nobody thought of it before!"

Chapter Two

Ma Rosie listened carefully as the boys told her of their plan. She seemed a bit doubtful at first, but after a while she agreed it was at least worth trying.

"Only take a few watermelons with you," she said. "If nobody buys a slice, then you can eat them yourselves as a reward."

The boys went with her into the field to choose the ripest and the juiciest-looking

watermelons. When they had
picked them, Ma Rosie put
them in a sack, and saw the
boys off on their way to the
hotel.

"Good luck!" she called out
as they set off.

The boys walked back into

town, towards the large hotel.
It was one of the best hotels in
that part of the country,
surrounded by wide green
lawns and with a swimming-

pool in the gardens. The hotel
guests often sat around the
pool, enjoying the sunshine.
Misipo was sure that they
would enjoy themselves even

more if they had a large, juicy
slice of watermelon!

Misipo and Sepo began to
walk up the drive of the hotel.
They had not gone far,

though, before they heard a
shout behind them. They
looked around, and saw one
of the hotel guards sitting
under a tree.

"Come here," he called out.
"Where do you think you're
going?"

Misipo and Sepo walked
over to the guard and told
him, quite politely, that they
were going to sell watermelons.

"Oh no, you're not," snorted
the guard. "We don't allow
people to pester the guests."

"But we won't be pestering them," protested Misipo. "We're only going to offer them some watermelon."

"Don't argue with me," said the guard angrily. "Get out of here! Right now!"

The boys walked back to the road, angry at the way the guard had treated them.

"I don't see why we shouldn't offer watermelon to the guests," said Misipo. "It's not doing anybody any harm."

"That's right," said Sepo. He

paused. "Why don't we try to get in anyway?"

"How?" asked Misipo.

Sepo pointed to the fence which ran round the grounds of the hotel.

"Just about every fence has

a hole in it," he said. "I'm sure we'll find one if we look for it!"

Sepo was right – there was a hole – and the two boys were soon running across lawns to

the poolside. Once there, they
took the biggest watermelon
from out of the sack, cut it up
neatly, and began to walk
round the pool, showing the
slices to the visitors.

One or two of the visitors were not interested, and shook their heads when the boys approached them. Most of them, though, licked their lips at the sight of the delicious

fruit, and readily paid the few
coins for a slice of cool
watermelon. Some people even
called the boys over for more.

Soon every watermelon had
been eaten and the sack was
quite empty. Misipo and Sepo,
their pockets full of money,

bundled up the sack and made their way back across the lawns to the fence. Their first day as watermelon sellers had been a very great success!

Chapter Three

Ma Rosie was delighted when the boys showed her how much money they had made. She wanted to share it with them, but Misipo shook his head.

"You can pay us in
watermelons," he said. "You
need that money for yourself."

The old woman was happy
to do this. She gave each boy
two watermelons to take away
with him, and it was agreed
that they would come back the
following Saturday to take
watermelons to the hotel.

"I hope I can grow enough,"
said Ma Rosie. "If you sell
them that quickly, I shall soon
have sold my entire crop!"

The boys returned, as
promised, the following
Saturday. Once again, Ma
Rosie showed them which
watermelons to pick, and they
carried these off in their sack.
Once again they slipped
through the hole in the fence,

cut up the watermelon, and began to offer it to the guests around the swimming-pool.

They had sold about half of their watermelons when they heard a shout from the direction of the hotel.

"Hey! You boys! Come here!" There was a man in a blue uniform running towards them.

Misipo looked nervously at Sepo. It was the hotel guard who had tried to stop them before. He was sure that they were in for trouble of some sort.

When the guard reached

them, he took Misipo by the
arm and gave him a shake.

"What are you doing here?"
he shouted. "Didn't I tell you
only the guests are allowed

here? Get out, right now! And
don't let me see you back
here, or you'll be sorry!"

"But we weren't doing any
harm," protested Misipo. "The

guests are enjoying our watermelons. Look!"

He was right, of course, but the guard was not interested.

"Out!" he shouted. "Out you go!"

Misipo and Sepo sadly made their way back to Ma Rosie's, their sack still half full of watermelons. They explained to her what had happened, and she shrugged her shoulders.

"I thought it was too good to last," she said. "Well, thank you anyway for trying for me, boys."

Misipo and Sepo walked home, carrying the two watermelons which Ma Rosie had given them as a present. They tried to think of any other way in which they could help their old friend. But it

seemed there was nothing
more they could do.

"It's so unfair," said Sepo.
"The guests really did enjoy
those watermelons. None of
them minded our being there."

They walked past the hotel

again. One of the other
guards was at the gate, and
he shook a finger at them in
warning. He must have been
told about them.

Then Misipo had an idea. It
was only an idea, and he was

not sure whether it could work, but he thought there was no harm in trying.

"If only we could speak to the manager," he said. "If we could explain to him how much the guests enjoyed the watermelons, I'm sure he would give us permission to sell them."

"He might," said Sepo. "But how do we get past the guards? They won't even allow us into the grounds."

"There may be a way," said Misipo. "Listen to this."

Sepo listened to his friend's plan. It sounded quite daring,

but he agreed that it might just work.

"But you say that we'll need Ma Rosie's help," he said. "Do you think she'll agree?"

"Let's ask her," said Misipo. "She might just say yes."

Chapter Four

The two boys went back to Ma Rosie's house and told her about their plan. She listened carefully, and then she smiled.

"That sounds rather exciting," she said.

"Do you mean you'll come with us?" asked Misipo, his voice high with excitement.

"Yes," said Ma Rosie. "As long as you walk slowly, I'll come."

Together with Ma Rosie,
the boys set off for the hotel
carrying two watermelons. It
took them a long time, as Ma
Rosie had to stop for a rest
from time to time. But

eventually they were there,
approaching the guard under
his tree.

"Why have you come back?"
he asked suspiciously. "We've

already had to chase you
away once today."

"We only came to talk to
you," said Misipo. "We saw
you sitting there in your

uniform and you looked a bit
hot. We thought you might
like some watermelon."

The guard looked at the
large watermelon Misipo was
holding. He was clearly
tempted. But was it against
the rules for him to eat
watermelon while on duty?

"Come on," encouraged Sepo. "It's really juicy, this one."

The guard looked again at

the watermelon and then
nodded.

"All right," he said. "Here.
You can use my penknife to
cut it."

Misipo cut out a large slice
and gave it to the guard to
eat. He bit into it hungrily,
the juice running down his
chin.

"Here you are," said
Misipo, after the guard had
finished. "Here's another
piece."

"Thank you," said the
guard gratefully. "I must say
this is the most delicious
watermelon I've ever tasted."

Misipo gave him a third
slice, and another slice after
that. At last the guard had
had enough, and he sat back
and smiled.

"That was wonderful," he
said. "Wonderful!"

"Good," said Ma Rosie.
"I'm glad you enjoyed it." She
paused. "But I'm sorry it's

made such a mess of your
uniform. Look! Hadn't you
better go and wash those
stains off quickly?"

The guard looked down at
his uniform and frowned.

"Now go along," said Ma Rosie sternly.

The guard did not think that he could argue with this determined old woman. Rather reluctantly, he got up

from his chair and walked
into a side entrance of the
hotel.

"It worked," said Misipo.
"Now's our chance."

Taking the other, uneaten
watermelon with them,
Misipo, Sepo and Ma Rosie
made their way across the

grass to the hotel. They were
not quite sure where to go,
but Ma Rosie stopped a
waitress who was walking
past and asked her to direct
them to the office. Once there,

they knocked loudly on the door, and a secretary called them in.

"Yes," she said, looking over her typewriter at her three unusual visitors. "What can we do for you?"

"We'd like to speak to the manager," said Ma Rosie. "Please. It's very important."

For a moment the secretary hesitated. Then she reached over and pressed a buzzer.

"You can go in," she said. "But please don't be long. He's a very busy man."

Misipo, Sepo and Ma Rosie entered the manager's office

and stood before his desk. He
looked at them quizzically,
wondering what an old
woman and two boys,
carrying a large watermelon,
could possibly want with him.

"I am a very old woman," began Ma Rosie, "but I still know how to grow good watermelons. Your guests love the delicious watermelons which these boys have been trying to sell to them. Please will you give us permission to sell them by the pool?"

The manager, who was a kind man, raised an eyebrow.

"Are you sure the guests
want them?" he said. "How
do you know they're so
delicious?"

"Try one," said Misipo. "If
you give me a knife I'll cut
you a slice."

The manager handed
Misipo a paper-knife and
watched, smiling, as he cut a
slice. Then Misipo passed the
slice to him, and he tried it,
his eyes opening wide with
pleasure.

"Mmm," he said. "That
certainly would taste even
better if you were sitting
beside the pool!"

He paused for a moment,
wiping the watermelon juice
off his chin.

"Very well," he said at last.

"You have my permission. I'll get one of my people to give each of you boys a white jacket and you can sell your watermelons here every Saturday afternoon. Will that do?"

Ma Rosie and the boys were delighted. The manager gave them a note to show to the guard at the gate. The guard was surprised, but he was very grateful when the boys gave him the rest of the watermelon.

"I shall eat it more carefully," he said. "I mustn't ruin my uniform again!"

Ma Rosie was very pleased
that everything had worked
out so well. The boys were
happy too. Their watermelon
slices were a great success with
the hotel guests and, what is
perhaps even more important,
there was always enough left
over for them at the end.

The guards at the hotel were also pleased. Misipo and Sepo always gave them a free slice of watermelon, and after a while they learned how to eat it without getting a single drop of juice on their uniforms. They were very proud of that!